TO THE CHILDREN WHO READ THIS BOOK

I have made this book especially for you; but not just for you, also for myself; not the present, grown-up self but the old self, the one left behind in childhood. In memory, I have gone back to those days and I have tried to recall some of the verses I learned and loved then, and have drawn them as I remember them. So there is nothing grown-up in this book, for all the time I was doing the drawings I was living again in my childhood, remembering the happy times as in *A Boy's Song*, and the sad times as in *The Lost Doll;* remembering how the countryside looked to me then, when, as in *Summer Morning*—

> "Along the clover-field I ran
>   To where the little wood began,
>   And there I understood at last
>   Why I had come so far, so fast—
>   On every leaf of every tree
>   A fairy sat and smiled at me! "

I have drawn them just as I saw them then!

Of course, I could not leave out the humorous poems, like the one about the Jumblies ("their heads are green and their hands are blue") who Went to Sea in a Sieve. And Lewis Carroll's *Thing-Um-A-Jig* who was one of that odd band of adventurers who went to hunt the Snark.

When I was little I loved the countryside, and illustrating the poems about nature has given me particular pleasure. I want to make *you* look again at things, always noticing something new which you missed at first—the shape of a leaf—the wonderful colours of berries and flowers—the birds and animals and insects—all there for you to see if you will stop a moment.

I remember with joy many such moments from *my* childhood and I have put all the thoughts and feelings which I had then into these drawings.

Hilda Boswell

HILDA BOSWELL'S
TREASURY *of* POETRY

Poems for Children
Selected and Illustrated by Hilda Boswell

LONDON   Collins   GLASGOW

CONTENTS

First Published 1968

FIRELIGHT

I LIKE to sit by the fire and stare
   At the curious things I can see in there;
It's better than pictures in a picture book
To sit by the fire and look, and look.

I can't see the things that Anne can see
(Anne, she's seven, but I'm just three)
Faces, and rivers, and forests, and all—
(Anne's enormous, but I'm quite small).

9

But the fire makes a nice sort of creaky song ;
It popples, as if it were running along ;
It talks quite soft, and it means to say,
" I know a nice quiet game to play."

I don't want to jump, and I don't want to shout ;
Mummy says, "What are you thinking about ? "
But I'm not thinking ; I just like to sit
Quite still by the fire, and stare at it.

WEE LITTLE HOUSE
WITH THE GOLDEN THATCH

WEE little house with the golden thatch ;
Twice I knocked and I lifted the latch :
"And pray, is the mistress here ? "
"In black stuff gown and a yellow vest,
She's busily packing her honey-chest ;
Will you taste a bit, my dear ? "

A PIPER

A PIPER in the streets to-day
    Set up and tuned and started to play,
And away, away, away on the tide
Of his music we started; on every side
Doors and windows were opened wide,
And men left down their work and came,
And women with petticoats coloured like flame.
And little bare feet that were blue with cold
Went dancing back to the age of gold,
For all the world went gay, went gay,
For half an hour in the street to-day.

SUMMER MORNING

THE air around was trembling bright
And full of dancing specks of light,
While butterflies were dancing too
Between the shining green and blue.
I might not watch, I might not stay,
I ran along the meadow way.

The straggling brambles caught my feet.
The clover-field was, oh! so sweet ;
I heard a singing in the sky,
And busy things went buzzing by;
And how it came I cannot tell,
But all the hedges sang as well.

Along the clover-field I ran
To where the little wood began,
And there I understood at last
Why I had come so far, so fast—
On every leaf of every tree
A fairy sat and smiled at me !

A WARBLER

IN the sedge a tiny song
Wells and trills the whole day long ;
In my heart another bird
Has its music heard.

As I watch and listen here,
Each to each pipes low and clear ;
But when one has ceased to sing,
Mine will still be echoing.

16

HERE A LITTLE CHILD
I STAND

HERE a little child I stand,
  Heaving up my either hand;
Cold as paddocks though they be;
Here I lift them up to Thee,
For a benison to fall
On our meat and on us all.

Amen.

17

THEY WENT TO SEA
IN A SIEVE

THEY went to sea in a Sieve, they did,
  In a Sieve they went to sea ;
In spite of all their friends could say,
On a winter's morn, on a stormy day,
    In a Sieve they went to sea!
And when the Sieve turned round and round,
And everyone cried, " You'll all be drowned !"
They cried aloud, " Our Sieve ain't big,
But we don't care a button, we don't care a fig !
    In a Sieve we'll go to sea ! "
Far and few, far and few,
Are the lands where the Jumblies live ;
Their heads are green and their hands are blue,
    And they went to sea in a Sieve.

They sailed away in a Sieve, they did,
  In a Sieve they sailed so fast,
With only a beautiful pea-green veil
Tied with a riband, by way of a sail,
  To a small tobacco-pipe mast ;
And everyone said who saw them go,
" Oh, won't they be soon upset, you know !
For the sky is dark, and the voyage is long,
And, happen what may, it's extremely wrong
  In a Sieve to sail so fast ! "

The water it soon came in, it did,
    The water it soon came in;
So to keep them dry they wrapped their feet
In a pinky paper all folded neat,
    And they fastened it down with a pin.
And they passed the night in a crockery jar,
And each of them said, "How wise we are!
Though the sky be dark, and the voyage be long,
Yet we never can think we were rash or wrong
    While round in our Sieve we spin!"

And all night long they sailed away ;
  And when the sun went down
They whistled and warbled a moony song,
To the echoing sound of a coppery gong,
  In the shade of the mountains brown.
" O Timballo ! How happy we are
When we live in a Sieve and a crockery jar,
And all night long in the moonlight pale
We sail away in a pea-green veil
  In the shade of the mountains brown ! "

They sailed to the Western Sea, they did,
        To a land all covered with trees,
And they bought an Owl, and a useful Cart,
And a pound of Rice, and a Cranberry Tart,
        And a hive of Silvery Bees.
And they bought a Pig, and some green Jackdaws,
And a lovely Monkey with lollipop paws,
And forty bottles of Ring-Bo-Ree,
        And no end of Stilton Cheese.

And in twenty years they all came back,
    In twenty years or more,
And everyone said, "How tall they've grown!"
For they've been to the Lakes, and the Torrible Zone,
    And the hills of the Chankly Bore!"

And they drank their health, and gave them a feast
Of dumplings made of beautiful yeast;
And everyone said, " If we only live,
We, too, will go to sea in a Sieve—
    To the hills of the Chankly Bore!"

Far and few, far and few,
    Are the lands where the Jumblies live ;
Their heads are green and their hands are blue,
    And they went to sea in a Sieve.

THE BUCKLE

I HAD a silver buckle,
   I sewed it on my shoe,
And 'neath a sprig of mistletoe
   I danced the evening through !

I had a bunch of cowslips,
   I hid them in a grot
In case the elves should come by night
   And me remember not.

I had a yellow riband,
    I tied it in my hair
That, walking in the garden,
    The birds might see it there.

I had a secret laughter,
    I laughed it near the wall :
Only the ivy and the wind
    May tell of it at all.

THE LAMB

LITTLE lamb who made thee ?
  Dost thou know who made thee ?
Gave thee life, and bade thee feed
By the stream and o'er the mead ;
Gave thee clothing of delight,
Softest clothing, woolly, bright ;
Gave thee such a tender voice,
Making all the vales rejoice ?
    Little lamb, who made thee ?
    Dost thou know who made thee ?

28

Little lamb, I'll tell thee ;
Little lamb, I'll tell thee :
He is calléd by thy name,
For He calls Himself a lamb,
He is meek and He is mild,
He became a little child.
I a child, and thou a lamb,
We are calléd by His name.
Little lamb, God bless thee !
Little lamb, God bless thee !

BOATS SAIL
ON THE RIVERS

BOATS sail on the rivers,
  And ships sail on the seas;
But clouds that sail across the sky
  Are prettier far than these.

There are bridges on the rivers,
  As pretty as you please ;
But the bow that bridges heaven,
  And overtops the trees,
And builds a road from earth to sky
  Is prettier far than these.

THE GARDEN YEAR

JANUARY brings the snow,
Makes our feet and fingers glow.

February brings the rain,
Thaws the frozen lake again.

March brings breezes, loud and shrill,
To stir the dancing daffodil.

April brings the primrose sweet,
Scatters daisies at our feet.

May brings flocks of pretty lambs
Skipping by their fleecy dams.

June brings tulips, lilies, roses,
Fills the children's hands with posies.

Hot July brings cooling showers,
Apricots, and gillyflowers.

August brings the sheaves of corn,
Then the harvest home is borne.

35

Warm September brings the fruit ;
Sportsmen then begin to shoot.

Fresh October brings the pheasant ;
Then to gather nuts is pleasant.

36

Dull November brings the blast ;
Then the leaves are whirling fast.

Chill December brings the sleet,
Blazing fire, and Christmas treat.

37

LAMBKIN AND SNOWDROP

THE lambkin tottering in its walk
With just a fleece to wear ;
The snowdrop drooping on its stalk
So slender—
Snowdrop and lamb, a pretty pair,
Braving the cold for our delight,
Both white,
Both tender.

THE LOST DOLL

I ONCE had a sweet little doll, dears,
    The prettiest doll in the world ;
Her cheeks were so red and so white, dears,
    And her hair was so charmingly curled.
But I lost my poor little doll, dears,
    As I played in the heath one day ;
And I cried for her more than a week, dears ;
    But I never could find where she lay.

I found my poor little doll, dears,
    As I played in the heath one day ;
Folks say she is terribly changed, dears,
    For her paint is all washed away,
And her arms trodden off by the cows, dears,
    And her hair not the least bit curled ;
Yet for old sakes' sake she is still, dears,
    The prettiest doll in the world.

THE MERMAID

Who would be
A mermaid fair,
Singing alone,
Combing her hair
Under the sea,
In a golden curl
With a comb of pearl,
On a throne ?

I would be a mermaid fair ;
I would sing to myself the whole of the day.
With a comb of pearl I would comb my hair ;
And still as I combed I would sing and say,
" Who is it loves me ? who loves not me ? "
I would comb my hair till my ringlets would fall,
        Low adown, low adown,
And I should look like a fountain of gold
        Springing alone
        With a shrill inner sound,
        Over the throne
        In the midst of the hall.

LIVING THINGS

HURT no living thing,
Ladybird, nor butterfly,
Nor moth with dusty wing,
Nor cricket chirping cheerily,
Nor grasshopper so light of leap,
Nor dancing gnat, nor beetle fat,
Nor harmless worms that creep.

THE BABES IN THE WOOD

MY DEAR, do you know,
How a long time ago,
Two poor little children
Whose names I don't know,
Were stolen away on a fine summer's day,
And left in a wood, as I've heard people say.

And when it was night,
So sad was their plight,
The sun it went down,
And the moon gave no light.
They sobbed and they sighed, and they bitterly cried,
And the poor little things, they lay down and died.

And when they were dead,
The Robins so red
    Brought strawberry-leaves
And over them spread ;
    And all the day long
    They sung them this song ;
"Poor babes in the wood! Poor babes in the wood!
And don't you remember the babes in the wood ? "

THE WINDS
THEY DID BLOW

THE winds they did blow;
The leaves they did wag;
Along came a beggar boy,
And put me in his bag.

He took me up to London ;
    A lady me did buy,
She put me in a silver cage,
    And hung me up on high,

With apples by the fire,
    And nuts for to crack,
Besides a little feather bed
    To rest my little back.

WYNKEN, BLYNKEN AND NOD

WYNKEN, Blynken, and Nod one night
     Sailed off in a wooden shoe,
Sailed on a river of crystal light
     Into a sea of dew.
" Where are you going, and what do you wish ? "
     The old Moon asked the three.
" We have come to fish for the herring fish
     That live in this beautiful sea ;
Nets of silver and gold have we,"
     Said Wynken,
     Blynken, and Nod.

The old Moon laughed and sang a song
   As they rocked in the wooden shoe ;
And the wind that sped them all night long
   Ruffled the waves of dew ;
The little stars were the herring fish
   That lived in that beautiful sea.
" Now cast your nets wherever you wish,
   But never afeared are we ! "
So cried the stars to the fishermen three,
     Wynken,
      Blynken, and Nod.

All night long their nets they threw
   For the fish in the twinkling foam,
Then down from the sky came the wooden shoe,
   Bringing the fishermen home ;
'Twas all so pretty a sail, it seemed
   As if it could not be ;
And some folk thought 'twas a dream they'd
     dreamed
   Of sailing that beautiful sea ;
But I shall name you the fishermen three,
    Wynken,
      Blynken, and Nod.

Wynken and Blynken are two little eyes,
    And Nod is a little head ;
And the wooden shoe that sailed the skies
    Is a wee one's trundle-bed.
So shut your eyes while Mother sings
    Of wonderful sights that be,
And you shall see the beautiful things
    As you rock in the misty sea
Where the old shoe rocked the fishermen three,
    Wynken,
        Blynken, and Nod.

SPRING

SOUND the flute !
    Now it's mute.
Birds delight
Day and night ;
Nightingale
In the dale,
Lark in sky,
Merrily,
Merrily, merrily to welcome in the year.

Little boy,
Full of joy ;
Little girl,
Sweet and small ;
Cock does crow,
So do you ;
Merry voice,
Infant noise,
Merrily, merrily to welcome in the year.

Little lamb,
Here I am ;
Come and lick
My white neck ;
Let me pull
Your soft wool;
Let me kiss
Your soft face :
Merrily, merrily, we welcome in the year.

THE LIGHTHEARTED FAIRY

OH, who is so merry, so merry, heigh ho !
As the light-hearted fairy ? heigh ho,
Heigh ho !
He dances and sings
To the sound of his wings
With a hey and a heigh and a ho !

Oh, who is so merry, so airy, heigh ho !
As the light-headed fairy ? heigh ho !
Heigh ho !
His nectar he sips
From the primroses' lips
With a hey and a heigh and a ho !

Oh, who is so merry, so merry, heigh ho !
As the light-footed fairy ? heigh ho !
Heigh ho !
The night is his noon
And the sun is his moon
With a hey and a heigh and a ho !

55

SWEET AND LOW

SWEET and low, sweet and low,
  Wind of the western sea,
Low, low, breathe and blow,
  Wind of the western sea !
  Over the rolling waters go,
  Come from the dying moon, and blow,
  Blow him again to me ;
While my little one, while my pretty one sleeps.

Sleep and rest, sleep and rest,
    Father will come to thee soon ;
Rest, rest, on mother's breast,
    Father will come to thee soon ;
    Father will come to his babe in the nest,
    Silver sails all out of the west
    Under the silver moon ;
Sleep, my little one, sleep, my pretty one, sleep.

THING-UM-A-JIG

"JUST the place for a Snark!" the Bellman cried,
  As he landed his crew with care;
Supporting each man on the top of the tide
  By a finger entwined in his hair.

" Just the place for a Snark ! I have said it twice :
That alone should encourage the crew.
Just the place for a Snark ! I have said it thrice :
What I tell you three times is true."

The crew was complete : it included a Boots—
A maker of Bonnets and Hoods—
A Barrister, brought to arrange their disputes—
And a Broker to value their goods.

There was one who was famed for the number
    of things
  He forgot when he entered the ship:
His umbrella, his watch, all his jewels and rings,
  And the clothes he had bought for the trip.

He had forty-two boxes, all carefully packed,
  With his name painted clearly on each :
But, since he omitted to mention the fact,
  They were all left behind on the beach.

The loss of his clothes hardly mattered, because
    He had seven coats on when he came,
With three pair of boots—but the worst of it was,
    He had wholly forgotten his name.

He would answer to " Hi ! " or to any loud cry,
    Such as " Fry me ! " or " Fritter my wig ! "
To "What you-may-call-um! " or "What-was-his-
        name ! "
    But especially " Thing-um-a-jig ! "

While, for those who preferred a more forcible word,
  He had different names from these :
His intimate friends called him " Candle-ends,"
  And his enemies " Toasted-cheese."

" His form is ungainly—his intellect small—"
  (So the Bellman would often remark)
" But his courage is perfect ! And that, after all,
  Is the thing that one needs with a Snark."

GRACE AT TABLE

OUR thankful prayer,
    Dear God, we say—
For all Thy blessings
    Day by day;

For earth and sky,
    For rain and sun,
For food and drink
    For everyone!

63

THE SONG OF THE ENGINE

WHEN you travel on the railway,
    And the line goes *up* a hill,
Just listen to the engine
    As it pulls you with a will.
Though it goes so very slowly
    It sings this little song,
" I *think* I can, I *think* I can,"
    And so it goes along.

64

But later on the journey,
  When you're going *down* a hill,
The train requires no pulling,
  And the engine's singing still.
If you listen very quietly
  You will hear this little song,
" I *thought* I could, I *thought* I could ! "
  And so it speeds along.

THE SPIDER
AND
THE FLY

"WILL you walk into my parlour?"
said the Spider to the Fly;
'Tis the prettiest little parlour that ever you did spy;
The way into my parlour is up a winding stair,
And I have many curious things to show
when you are there,"
" Oh, no, no," said the little Fly;
" to ask me is in vain;
For who goes up your winding stair
can ne'er come down again."

" I'm sure you must be weary, dear,
    with soaring up so high ;
Will you rest upon my little bed ? "
    said the Spider to the Fly.
" There are pretty curtains drawn around ;
    the sheets are fine and thin ;
And if you like to rest awhile,
    I'll snugly tuck you in ! "
" Oh, no, no," said the little Fly ; " for I've often
    heard it said,
They never wake again who sleep upon your bed! "

Said the cunning Spider to the Fly :
  " Dear friend, what can I do
To prove the warm affection
  I have *always* felt for you ?
I have within my pantry good store of all that's nice;
I'm sure you're very welcome—
  will you please to take a slice ? "
" Oh, no, no," said the little Fly ;
" kind sir, that cannot be ;
I've heard what's in your pantry,
  and I do not wish to see ! "

68

" Sweet creature ! " said the Spider,
    "you are witty and you're wise ;
How handsome are your gauzy wings,
    how brilliant are your eyes !
I have a little looking-glass
    upon my parlour shelf,
If you'll step in one moment, dear,
    you shall behold yourself."
" I thank you, gentle sir," she said,
    " for what you're pleased to say,
And bidding you good-morning now,
    I'll call another day. . . . "

SANTA CLAUS

HE comes in the night! He comes in the night!
   He softly, silently comes;
While the little brown heads on the pillows so white
Are dreaming of bugles and drums.
He cuts through the snow like a whip through the
   foam,
While the white flakes around whirl;
Who tells him I know not, but he findeth the home
Of each good little boy and girl.

His sleigh it is long, and deep, and wide;
It will carry a host of things,
While dozens of drums hang over the side,
With the sticks sticking under the strings.
And yet not the sound of a drum is heard,
Not a bugle blast is blown,
As he mounts to the chimney-top like a bird,
And drops to the earth like a stone.

The little red stockings he silently fills,
Till the red stockings will hold no more ;
The bright little sleds for the great snow hills
Are quickly set down on the floor.
Then Santa Claus mounts to the roof like a bird,
And glides to his seat in the sleigh ;
Not the sound of a bugle or drum is heard
As he noiselessly gallops away.

He rides to the East, and he rides to the West,
Of his goodies he touches not one;
He eateth the crumbs of the Christmas feast
When the dear little folks are done.
Old Santa Claus doeth all he can;
This beautiful mission is his;
Then, children, be good to the little old man,
When you find who the little man is.

LITTLE
BLUE
PIGEON

SLEEP little pigeon, and fold your wings,
    Little blue pigeon with velvet eyes ;
Sleep to the singing of mother-bird swinging,
    Swinging the nest where her little one lies.

Away out yonder I see a star,
    Silvery star with a tinkling song ;
To the soft dew falling I hear it calling,
    Calling and tinkling the night along.

In through the window a moonbeam comes,
    Little gold moonbeam with misty wings ;
All silently creeping, it asks : " Is he sleeping,
    Sleeping and dreaming while mother sings ? "

Up from the sea there floats the sob
    Of the waves that are breaking upon the shore,
As though they were groaning in anguish,
        and moaning ;
    Bemoaning the ship that shall come no more.

But sleep, little pigeon, and fold your wings,
    Little blue pigeon with mournful eyes ;
Am I not singing ? See, I am swinging ;
    Swinging the nest where my darling lies.

THE WRAGGLE TAGGLE GYPSIES

THREE gypsies stood at the Castle gate,
     They sang so high, they sang so low,
The lady sate in her chamber late,
Her heart it melted away as snow.

They sang so sweet, they sang so shrill,
That fast her tears began to flow.
And she laid down her silken gown,
Her golden rings and all her show.

She plucked off her high-heeled shoes,
A' made of Spanish leather, O!
She would in the street, with her bare, bare feet,
All out in the wind and weather, O!

It was late last night, when my lord came home,
Enquiring for his a-lady, O!
The servants said on every hand,
"She's gone with the wraggle taggle gypsies, O!

"O saddle to me my milk-white steed.
Go fetch me my pony, O!
That I may ride and seek my bride,
Who is gone with the wraggle taggle gypsies, O!"

O he rode high and he rode low,
He rode through woods and copses too.
Until he came to an open field,
And there he espied his a-lady, O!

"What makes you leave your house and land?
What makes you leave your money, O?
What makes you leave your new-wedded lord,
To go with the wraggle taggle gypsies, O? "

"What care I for my house and land ?
What care I for my money, O?
What care I for my new-wedded lord?
I'm off with the wraggle taggle gypsies, O!"

" Last night you slept on a goose-feather bed,
With the sheet turned down so bravely, O!
And to-night you'll sleep in a cold open field,
Along with the wraggle taggle gypsies, O! "

" What care I for a goose-feather bed,
With the sheet turned down so bravely, O?
For to-night I shall sleep in a cold open field,
Along with the wraggle taggle gypsies, O! "

THE FLOWER SELLER

THE Flower Seller's fat and she wears a big shawl,
She sits on the kerb with her basket and all ;
The wares that she sells us are not very dear,
And are always the loveliest things of the year.

Daffodils in April,
Purple Flags in May,
Sweet Peas like butterflies
Upon a summer's day,
Brown leaves in autumn,
Green leaves in spring,
And berries in the winter
When the carol singers sing.

The Flower Seller sits with her hands in her lap,
When she's not crying Roses, she's taking a nap ;
Her bonnet is queer, and she calls you My Dear,
And sells you the loveliest things of the year.

NOD

SOFTLY along the road of evening,
  In a twilight dim with rose,
Wrinkled with age, and drenched with dew
  Old Nod, the shepherd, goes.

His drowsy flock streams on before him,
  Their fleeces charged with gold,
To where the sun's last beam leans low
  On Nod the shepherd's fold.

The hedge is quick and green with briar ;
From their sand the conies creep ;
And all the birds that fly in heaven
Flock singing home to sleep.

His lambs outnumber a noon's roses,
Yet, when night's shadows fall,
His blind old sheep-dog, Slumber-soon,
Misses not one of all.

His are the quiet steeps of dreamland,
The waters of no-more-pain,
His ram's bell rings 'neath an arch of stars,
" Rest, rest, and rest again."

SLEEP, BABY, SLEEP

SLEEP, baby, sleep,
 Our cottage vale is deep ;
The little lamb is on the green,
With woolly fleece so soft and clean—
 Sleep, baby, sleep !

Sleep, baby, sleep,
Down where the woodbines creep ;
Be always like the lamb so mild,
A kind and sweet and gentle child
 Sleep, baby, sleep !

GOD BE IN MY HEAD

GOD be in my head,
　　And in my understanding;

God be in my eyes,
　　And in my looking;

God be in my mouth,
　　And in my speaking;

God be at mine end,
　　And at my departing.

THE KITTEN
AT PLAY

SEE the kitten on the wall,
    Sporting with the leaves that fall,
Withered leaves—one, two, and three—
From the lofty elder tree !
Through the calm and frosty air
Of this morning bright and fair,
Eddying round and round they sink
Softly, slowly: one might think
From the motions that are made,
Every little leaf conveyed
Sylph or faery hither tending,
To this lower world descending,
Each invisible and mute,
In his wavering parachute.
—But the kitten, how she starts,
Crouches, stretches, paws, and darts !
First at one, and then its fellow,
Just as light and just as yellow ;
There are many now—now one—
Now they stop ; and there are none.

SOMEWHERE

COULD you tell me the way to Somewhere ?
Somewhere, Somewhere,
I have heard of a place called Somewhere—
But know not where it can be.
It makes no difference,
Whether or not
I go in dreams
Or trudge on foot :
Would you tell me the way to Somewhere,
The Somewhere meant for me ?

There's a little old house in Somewhere—
    *Some*where, *Some*where,
A queer little house, with a Cat and a Mouse—
    Just room enough for three.
        A kitchen, a larder,
        A bin for bread,
        A string for candles,
        Or stars instead,
        A table, a chair,
        And a four-post bed—
There's room for us all in Somewhere,
    For the Cat and the Mouse and Me.

A BOY'S SONG

WHERE the pools are bright and deep,
Where the grey trout lies asleep,
Up the river and o'er the lea,
That's the way for Billy and me.

Where the blackbird sings the latest,
Where the hawthorn blooms the sweetest,
Where the nestlings chirp and flee,
That's the way for Billy and me.

Where the mowers mow the cleanest,
Where the hay lies thick and greenest,
There to track the homeward bee,
That's the way for Billy and me.

Where the hazel bank is steepest
Where the shadow falls the deepest,
Where the clustering nuts fall free,
That's the way for Billy and me . . .

GOLDEN SLUMBERS

GOLDEN slumbers kiss your eyes,
    Smiles awake you when you rise.
Sleep, pretty wantons, do not cry,
And I will sing a lullaby.
Rock them, rock them, lullaby.

Care is heavy, therefore sleep you ;
You are care, and care must keep you.
Sleep, pretty wantons, do not cry,
And I will sing a lullaby :
Rock them, rock them, lullaby.

EXTREMES

A LITTLE boy once played so loud
That the Thunder, up in a thunder-cloud,
Said : " Since I can't be heard, why, then
I'll never, never thunder again ! "

And a little girl once kept so still
That she heard a Fly on the window-sill
Whisper and say to a Ladybird :
" She's the silliest child I ever heard ! "

MRS. PECK PIGEON

MRS. Peck Pigeon
Is picking for bread ;
Bob, bob, bob,
    Goes her little round head.

Tame as a pussy cat
    In the street,
Step, step, step,
    Go her little red feet.

With her little red feet
    And her little round head
Mrs. Peck Pigeon
    Goes picking for bread.

MICE

I THINK mice
Are rather nice.

Their tails are long,
Their faces small,
They haven't any
Chins at all.

Their ears are pink,
Their teeth are white,
They run about
The house at night.

They nibble things
They shouldn't touch
And no one seems
To like them much.

But I think mice
Are nice.

THE BUTTERFLY'S BALL

COME, take up your hats, and away let us haste
To the Butterfly's ball and the Grasshopper's
feast ;
The trumpeter Gadfly has summoned the crew,
And the revels are now only waiting for you.

On the smooth-shaven grass by the side of the wood,
Beneath a broad oak that for ages has stood,
See the children of earth and the tenants of air
For an evening's amusement together repair.

And there came the Beetle, so blind and so black,
Who carried the Emmet, his friend, on his back ;
And there was the Gnat, and the Dragonfly too,
With all their relations, green, orange, and blue.

And there came the Moth in his plumage of down,
And the Hornet in jacket of yellow and brown,
Who with him the Wasp, his companion, did bring,
But they promised that evening to lay by their sting.

And the shy little Dormouse crept out of his hole,
And led to the feast his blind brother the Mole ;
And the Snail, with his horns peeping out from
    his shell,
Came from a great distance—the length of an ell.

A mushroom, their table, and on it was laid
A water dock leaf, which a table-cloth made ;
The viands were various, to each of their taste,
And the Bee brought his honey to crown the repast.

There close on his haunches, so solemn and wise,
The Frog from a corner looked up to the skies ;
And the Squirrel, well pleased such diversion to see,
Sat cracking his nuts overhead in a tree.

Then out came the Spider, with fingers so fine,
To show his dexterity on the tight line :
From one branch to another his cobwebs he slung,
Then as quick as an arrow he darted along.

But just in the middle, oh ! shocking to tell !
From his rope in an instant poor Harlequin fell ;
Yet he touched not the ground, but with talons
    outspread,
Hung suspended in air at the end of a thread.

Then the Grasshopper came with a jerk and a spring,
Very long was his leg, though but short was his
        wing ;
He took but three leaps, and was soon out of sight,
Then chirped his own praises the rest of the night.

With step so majestic the Snail did advance,
And promised the gazers a minuet to dance;
But they all laughed so loud that he pulled in his
    head,
And went in his own little chamber to bed.

Then as evening gave way to the shadows of night,
The watchman, the Glow-worm, came out with
    his light;
Then home let us hasten while yet we can see,
For no watchman is waiting for you and for me.

A FAIRY WENT A-MARKETING

A FAIRY went a-marketing—
    She bought a little fish ;
She put it in a crystal bowl
    Upon a golden dish.
An hour she sat in wonderment
    And watched its silver gleam,
And then she gently took it up
    And slipped it in a stream.

A fairy went a-marketing—
    She bought a coloured bird ;
It sang the sweetest, shrillest song
    That ever she had heard.
She sat beside its painted cage
    And listened half the day,
And then she opened wide the door
    And let it fly away.

A fairy went a-marketing—
　　She bought a winter gown
All stitched about with gossamer
　　And lined with thistledown.
She wore it all the afternoon
　　With prancing and delight,
Then gave it to a little frog
　　To keep him warm at night.

A fairy went a-marketing—
    She bought a gentle mouse
To take her tiny messages,
    To keep her little house.
All day she kept its busy feet
    Pit-patting to and fro,
And then she kissed its silken ears,
    Thanked it, and let it go.

THE PRETTY BIRD

MARY had a pretty bird
  With feathers bright and yellow—
Slender legs—upon my word—
  He *was* a pretty fellow.

THE CAT SAT ASLEEP

THE cat sat asleep by the fire,
  The mistress snored loud as a pig,
Jack took up his fiddle by Jenny's desire
And struck up a bit of a jig.

GRASSHOPPER GREEN

GRASSHOPPER Green is a comical chap ;
　He lives on the best of fare.
Bright little trousers, jacket and cap,
　These are his summer wear.
Out in the meadow he loves to go,
　Playing away in the sun ;
It's hopperty, skipperty, high and low,
　Summer's the time for fun.

Grasshopper Green has a quaint little house ;
    It's under the hedge so gay.
Grandmother Spider, as still as a mouse,
    Watches him over the way.
Gladly he's calling the children, I know,
    Out in the beautiful sun ;
It's hopperty, skipperty, high and low,
    Summer's the time for fun.

HOPPER
COT

LITTLE ROBIN

COME here, little robin, and don't be afraid,
   I would not hurt even a feather ;
Come here, little robin, and pick up some bread,
   To feed you this very cold weather.

The winter has come, but it will not stay long,
   And summer we soon shall be greeting ;
Then remember, dear robin, to sing me a song
   In return for the breakfast you're eating.

GLAD

THE rose is on the tree,
  The blackbird sings to me,
The poppy's in the corn ;
I'm glad that I was born.

The clouds are sailing high,
The lark is in the sky,
The wind is big and wild ;
I'm glad that I'm a child.

Glad that I can run
And play beneath the sun,
Until I fall asleep,
Wrapped in darkness deep.

OLD SHELLOVER

"COME ! " said Old Shellover.
     "What ? " says Creep.
" The horny old Gardener's fast asleep ;
The fat cock Thrush
To his nest has gone ;
And the dew shines bright
In the rising Moon ;
Old Sallie Worm from her hole doth peep ;
" Come ! " said old Shellover.
" Ay ! " said Creep.

BEDTIME

THE evening is coming,
  The sun sinks to rest ;
The rooks are all flying
  Straight home to the nest,
" Caw ! " says the rook, as he flies overhead,
" It's time little people were going to bed ! "

The flowers are closing ;
　　The daisy's asleep,
The primrose is buried
　　In slumber so deep.
Shut up for the night is the pimpernel red ;
It's time little people were going to bed !

The butterfly drowsy,
　　Has folded its wing ;
The bees are returning,
　　No more the birds sing.
Their labour is over, their nestlings are fed ;
It's time little people were going to bed !

Here comes the pony,
    His work is all done ;
Down through the meadow
    He takes a good run ;
Up go his heels, and down goes his head ;
It's time little people were going to bed !

Good night, little people,
    Good night and good night ;
Sweet dreams to your eyelids
    Till dawning of light ;
The evening has come, there's no more to be said,
It's time little people were going to bed !

ACKNOWLEDGEMENTS

For kind permission to include copyright material, the compiler and publishers of this book offer their thanks to the following:

Messrs. Blackie & Son, Ltd. for "Song of the Engine" from *In Poem Town* by Christine Weatherly. Miss Eleanor Farjeon and Messrs. Michael Joseph Ltd. for "The Flower Seller" from *Sing for your Supper* and "Mrs. Peck Pigeon" from *Silver Sand and Snow*. The Literary Trustees of Walter de la Mare and The Society of Authors as their representative for "The Buckle", "Nod", "Old Shellover", "Somewhere" and "A Warbler" by Walter de la Mare. Messrs. F. Muller for "Firelight" and "Glad" from *Six O'Clock And After* by Irene and Aubrey de Selincourt. The Society of Authors as the literary representative of the Estate of the late Miss Rose Fyleman for "A Fairy Went A-Marketing", "Mice" and "Summer Morning" by Rose Fyleman. Mrs. Estella Starkey for "A Piper" by Seumas O'Sullivan.

Although every effort has been made to trace the copyright holders, in a few cases this has proved impossible. Should any omissions be noticed, it is hoped that the publishers will be informed so that acknowledgements may be made in future editions.